CW01635107

This Isn't Just a Game Series Presents:

Where's My Stick?

Book One

by

Cameron Huber

KidPub Press
Boston

Published by KidPub Press
www.kidpub.com

ISBN: 978-1-61018-199-0
Printed in USA

I would like to dedicate this book to my lacrosse team and family.
Thank you.

Contents

Chapter 1

The Championship is Here

"KIRA! KIRA! KIRA! LET'S GO CRAZY STICKS!" ALL THE FANS SCREAMED out in the stands. I was at this scary moment standing right in the center of the field. All I could hear at this moment was my heart racing. BOOM! BOOM! BOOM! I gazed up at the big round sun. I needed to relax and breathe in the oxygen, breathe out.

I started to glance at the huge crowd and look for the one person I needed, my best friend. Even though my mom was there, I knew she was my biggest fan. My mom always gave me support, even if she was a little mad at me. But I really need to talk to my best friend. She knew what to do whenever I would ever get this anxious.

"Where is she?" I thought nervously. My game was starting in about fifteen minutes. I was as nervous as a prey when it sees its predator. Oh, I forgot to mention, I am Kira Alexandra. I love lacrosse, and I have brown hair, with brown eyes. I have really boring features, or that is what I think. My mom doesn't though. But what's new? All parents give their children courage, which is like their job. I go to St. Matthew's in Maine. And right now I am playing lacrosse, the world's best sport started by the boy Indians, at the nearby high school. The one my older brother goes to.

"Kira!" a familiar voice shouted.

"Please be Ana. Please be Ana!" I pleaded hoping it was my best friend. I quickly spun around and saw it was my teammate Jesse.

"Kira! Coach Maddy wants to see you in the high school!" Jesse told me out of breath.

Then another one of my teammates, Jilly, came dashing towards me and told me the same thing. "Oh, Kira. I'm so glad I found you. Coach Maddy wants to see you," Jilly repeated.

"Why is she in there?" I wondered.

"Earth to Kira, yo! Coach Maddy wants to see you!" Jilly screamed a little too loud at me.

"I know Jilly, but thanks anyway. I'll go find her right now," I said smoothly while putting down my stick and ignoring that rude comment. I started to run into the crowd, not paying attention to Ana who was right next to me. I sprang into the high school. "Hello? Is anyone here? Coach Maddy?"

"Hello, there. Kira. I've been waiting for you," a Mysterious Voice calls out.

"What the...? Who's there?" I reply getting nervous.

"It's better that I'm just...a person who shall be unnamed. But, you know me," the voice answered.

"Really, who are you? And where is Coach Maddy?" I questioned.

"Kira? Kira? Where are you?" someone else called.

"We will meet again, Kira," the Mysterious Voice whispers and then disappeared.

"Kira! There you are! I was looking all over for you!" I turn around and see it is Ana. Finally! "I was trying to get your attention in the crowd! I guess you didn't see me. That doesn't matter right now, though. Because you should be on the field! Your game starts in like ten minutes!"

"Oh, Ana! Finally I found you! I was so worried! Did you just see that odd person? Who ever it was, sounded oddly similar to one of my teammates," I sighed with relief and a little confusion.

"No..." Ana gave me a strange look. "You're supposed to be on the field! You are center, the most important position!"

"Well my coach wanted to see me here. Have you seen Coach Maddy?"

"No, I've gotta go back to my seat with your mom. Good luck out there!" Ana smiled and sprinted out the door.

"Kira? Is that you? It's Coach Maddy," and then Coach Maddy appeared from behind the corner.

"Oh, hello Coach Maddy. I'm here, just like you wanted me to be," I grin, with a little bit of pressure about what Ana said. "You are center! The most important position!" the words whisper in my ears over and over again.

"Yes, Kira. I wanted to talk to you about the game today, but in private because some of your teammates might have gotten jealous if I did in front of them. I know you love lacrosse, and I wanted to reward you for always being a great teammate and for doing a good job this season so far. So, here."

Coach Maddy handed me a jersey that said "Captain."

"Wow, Coach Maddy. I wasn't expecting this. Thank you so much!" I exclaim. I was speechless. Frozen, actually.

"Kira, dear. Are you ok?" Coach Maddy questioned very concerned.

"I can't believe I am captain! Now the pressure is really, truly on me!"

"Kira?" Coach Maddy asks.

"Huh? Oh, thank you so, so much Coach Maddy! I won't let you and the rest of the team down!" I encouraged.

"You're very welcome, Kira. Now let's hustle and get out there!" Coach Maddy walked with me out of the huge high school and onto the field.

"Ok, now Coach Maddy, let's win the championship game for this season and win the big trophy!" I exclaim and run towards my precious, valuable stick. It is my good luck charm for games.

But for some reason it wasn't there.

"Um, Jilly? Do you still have that extra stick? My stick…umm, lost its strings. Can I borrow it?" I ask hoping for a "yes."

"Sure Kira. I don't know how yours could lose its strings, but how should I know? I am just dumb, and you are all smart!" Jilly responded fresh like she was mad at me. Then while Jilly was putting in her mouth guard, she gave me the stick. "Oh, and what did Coach Maddy want you for?" Jilly asks like she knew the answer.

"Oh, just wanted to say great job this season and good luck on the game," I thought of quickly. But I wasn't such a good liar.

"Well, why did she just say it to YOU only?" Jilly started to get annoyed.

"No idea," I spit out. And then I ran on the field.

"Well, I hope we LOSE!" Jilly whispers to herself.

And those words scared me. Literally.

Chapter 2

Game Over

"AAAAHHHH!" I SCREAMED FALLING ONTO THE COLD, MUDDY FIELD. I saw stars. In that second, I didn't know what happened. What I did notice was someone made my lacrosse stick's strings extra-long, and they tripped me. "OW!!!" I scream! Tears are pouring down my face.

The crowd gasps. My mom comes sprinting onto the field. Thankfully, someone in the crowd is a doctor. It turns out I can't play in the game. I twisted my ankle really badly, but thankfully it didn't break. But it was very close to breaking. I needed to sit in the crowd with crutches. Unfortunately again, I needed to be on crutches for two weeks.

"No! I have to play! I'll be letting my team down!" The tears burst from my eyes. And from the corner of my water filled eyes, I saw Coach Maddy handing Jilly the captain's jersey and saw Jilly's smirk. This was all her fault! I shook my head as the doctor wrapped up my foot.

My mom carried me into the stands. I just sat in her arms, shocked. The rest was a blur, for I was too upset to watch. I remembered only one horrible thing. Jilly looked me dead in the eye and said she didn't do it. And right after that, she grabbed the stick out of my hands, and I saw the extra strings in her bag. Why would she do that, and why did she lie right to my face? But before that, when I was in the stands, I saw the mysterious person in a black cloak, looking right at me.

The good news was that we won. But really, I lost. I let my team down. And I lost my stick! My stick! MY LUCKY CHARM! That's probably why I got injured. But that is no biggy. I think first I need to figure out who Mysterious Voice is...Who could it be, and why?

Chapter 3

What is Going On?

THE NEXT DAY AT SCHOOL WAS NOT LIKE MY NORMAL SCHOOL DAY. SINCE everyone on my team goes to my school, rumors have been spreading about me trying to get all the attention and about me being rude to teammates and also that I was mad at Jilly for her getting the captain's jersey instead of me.

Well, I *was* a little upset, but I was not angry at her. And thankfully no one knew that I had the jersey first, and then that accident and then Jilly got it. But unfortunately at school, every time I would see a teammate, they would just give me a dirty look and start to whisper. I can't believe Jilly started this, and we won the championship! Doesn't anyone care about that? Well, technically, they won. I lost.

"Hey, Jesse. Did you hear? Kira thinks she's the best lacrosse player! And she was so angry at me for getting the captain's jersey! And she blamed me for her tripping! I thought she was supposed to be a nice teammate! But, she is not anymore!" Jilly whispers too loudly so all my teammates heard.

And that is how the big rumor started spreading, all by one girl named Jilly Tent.

What is really funny is that I and Jilly used to be best friends when we were little. But that all changed, on my first day of second grade. Ana was my best friend since we were babies, but in kindergarten, she moved away. We did face chat that our moms set up, and we emailed each other. So while she was away, me and Jilly became best friends. After school everyday, my mom had to work. So I would go over her house and we would play with our Barbie dolls. And so on the first day of second grade, Ana came back. I was so excited and played with her. Jilly got so angry at me, she would not talk to me. And if she did talk to me, Jilly would say something rude or make rumors. So she has been keeping a grudge for three-and-a-half years. And if your best friend moved away, and she came back, wouldn't you be so happy and play with her? And also, don't you think three-and-a-half years is a long time to be holding a grudge?

When I finally got home from a hard day of school, my mom comforted me.

"Hey honey. How was your day at school?" My mom always asks when I get off the bus while she's making a salad. The usual schedule.

"Not good at all. Ever since I got the jersey, and lost it, Coach Maddy wanted to see me, the accident, and I told Jilly...WAIT! Mom! Did you get my stick?" I started to get worried like when a kid gets picked on by a bully.

"No. I never knew you lost your stick. Do you think someone accidentally took it?" my mom gets up and calls my dad while I make a list in my head of some suspects:

Jilly, Jesse, other teammates, like who or MYSTERIOUS VOICE!

"Mom! Mom! I know who did it!" I quickly moved on my crutches into my mom's bedroom.

"Who took it?" my mom questioned.

"MYSTERIOUS VOICE!" I scream.

"Who?" my mom asks while she looks at me like I have ten heads.

"Ok, so before I ran into Ana and Coach Maddy, there was someone in the high school. Whoever it was, they tried to freak me out. The Mysterious Voice was really rude. Probably he/she did it! But who and why?" I ask my mom.

"Honey, maybe whoever took your stick probably thought it was theirs," my mom tried to think of what else to say.

"No. My stick has my name and address on it. This wasn't any accident. You know that that stick is special. It's like my good luck charm. Grandma gave me it! Yesterday I couldn't play because of that accident! Bad luck!" I followed my mom out of her room.

"I'm sorry sweetie. We have to buy you a new one. I'm sorry," my mom says as she picks up her magazine.

"I'm sorry Mom. I have to get my stick. And figure out who stole it," I say determined to figure out the mystery like Sherlock Holmes.

All afternoon I thought and thought about who did it. Who would steal someone's lacrosse stick? I need it. It had to be someone who knew that the stick was my good luck charm. So that narrowed it to the people I started with. Jilly, Jesse, or Mysterious Voice. Ana would NEVER do that to me. Would she?

At dinner, I told my big brother, Toby, who goes to the high school. I told him how I almost played yesterday before that whole accident happened, and I told my dad about what happened yesterday and then today.

"Well, congratulations honey on the championship, and I'm sorry about your leg, losing your lucky stick, and what happened at school. Kids can be like that sometimes. Maybe they are just jealous because you are really good at lacrosse," my dad responded.

"Or maybe they are just jerks," my brother responded.

To change the subject, my mom said, "Isn't this food yummy? It was Grandma's special recipe that she would make when I was upset like you."

"Yes, I remember you telling me that. And this food is very delicious, honey," my dad responded before he shoved a whole piece of chicken into his mouth.

"It's alright," my brother responded staring at his food like he usually does. That's my older brother for you. He is a high school boy who is shy, and tries to act cool. He has black hair and always wears dark clothes. He is a little too quiet. Sometimes it feels like I'm an only child, because my brother is always out with his friends or just outside in town walking around, awkwardly.

"I love this food Mom," I reply while staring at Toby. Something about him today is different, like something changed.

"Toby, why do you like to stare at your food?" my dad questions as he pokes Toby. "Son? Are you alive? Hee hee."

My dad loves to fool around. Just like my grand pop. You know the old saying, "Like father, like son," that's what it's like for my grand pop and dad.

So after I ate dinner, put the dishes in the sink, and cleaned the dishes, I followed my brother and eavesdropped on him. I saw him putting a black cloak over his round face. And he had a big smile on his face as he searched through his closet, looking for his backpack.

Then all of a sudden, while I was gathering thoughts, I was interrupted by the phone when it rang.

"Hello, I've been doing what you have told me," my brother told the person on the other end of the phone.

"Good, did you get the stuff I asked for?" the deep voice questioned my brother.

"Um, yes. I got the—"Toby got interrupted.

ACHOO! Curse my loud sneezing. Whoops!

"Kira? Are you spying on me?" Toby asks annoyed taking off the cloak and walking out of the door into the hallway.

I quickly galloped into my room on my crutches and pretended to read a magazine.

He stepped into my room, and gave me a funny look.

"What?" I ask nicely like I don't know anything. But, yet again, I am not a good liar.

"I know you heard me. Now, I am either going to tell on you and be so happy, or tell you the truth since you might have heard too much. How much did you hear?" my brother asks like a serious judge.

"Well," I began to say. "A little bit…sort of…well…um…"

"Spit it out!" Toby angrily demands. "Tell me how much you heard!"

"All of it," I mumble.

"You…. You!" Toby started to get steam out of his ears. "I am going to get killed! My boss is going to kill me!" Toby muttered.

"Who is your boss?" I ask quietly.

"What? You did this to me! Because of you, my secret job is going to get ruined!" my brother explodes with anger.

"I can help," I offered.

"No! You have done too much damage! Thanks a lot! I wish you weren't alive!" Toby screams and runs out of my room full of madness. To make things worse, my mom comes up and yells at both of us.

That night, I keep repeating the words Toby said. "I wish you weren't alive!" And I had a dream about me in heaven, not being alive. I had no family, no nothing.

The next morning, I couldn't take it. I had to talk to Toby. Was he the Mysterious Voice? Or was he working for Mysterious Voice? I had so many questions.

Knock, knock!

"Go away!" Toby muttered. "You ruined my life!"

"Just let me come in, to make things clear! I need to talk to you!" I constantly yell in the hallway until he finally answers.

"What?!" he asks madly with his hair all over his face.

"Were you the person in that black cloak at my championship game?" I question like a news reporter.

"Um….. I have no idea what you are talking about," Toby lied closing the door.

"Oh, brother! Yes you do! You know what I am talking about!" I snap.

"Oh my gosh! Just go away!" Toby yells.

"Not until you let me in and tell me what was that stuff yesterday!" I respond.

"What do you want to know…?" Toby whispers through a crack in the door.

"Who was in the high school before I was with Coach Maddy?" I ask.

"Somebody in a black cloak with a deep voice and a small head," was Toby's response.

I never mentioned anything about a small head…

And then things got serious. Quickly, I ask Toby tons of questions. And each answer comes with more hints. Like, blackish brown hair, small head, tall, was at my house before. So that left a few different options. But it all came down to the last question…

"Were you the person in the black cloak, or do you work for the person in the black cloak?" I ask him.

"Um...I can't say that information...my boss will get mad," Toby mutters.

"A ha! You said boss! So you do work for mysterious cloak person!" I point at Toby.

"Um...maybe!" Toby whispers looking at his black shoes.

I am making some progress!

Chapter 4

Who is the Mysterious Voice?

FINALLY, IT IS MORNING AGAIN. *TIME TO FIGURE OUT WHERE THE HECK MY STICK is!* I think to myself, while brushing my teeth. I quickly hop on my crutches onto the school bus and takeout my new notebook. I write "Operation: who stole my stick. And who is Mysterious Voice. First ask Ana for help."

I once again think about the suspects. *Jilly, Jesse, Mysterious Voice.* I didn't think it would be Jesse. She's too nice, and she didn't believe the rumors. She's a true teammate. So now the suspects are Jilly or Mysterious Voice. But since Toby told me he worked for Mysterious Voice, he can't be working for a kid who is younger than he is! That would be funny though. So now it is just Mysterious Voice. *Who is it?* I keep repeating in my head until we are at school.

I dash right for Ana, who is saying goodbye to her mom. "Ana! Ana! I need you! Pronto!" I scream jumping with my crutches as fast as I can towards her.

"What? What's so important?" she responds a little annoyed.

“Someone stole my stick. It was either Jilly, but I don’t really see a good chance of that, or that strange person I was talking about before my game on Sunday. I need your help to figure out who did it. And if it was Mysterious Voice, who that person actually is,” I respond as I wait for an answer.

Ana just stares at me. Her jaw drops to the ground. “Girl, you need help!” she responds as she pushes me through the door.

We start thinking of how to figure out if it is Jilly or Mysterious Voice. We come up with Jilly had an extra stick that looked exactly like mine! So, we’re going to ask her. When we see her, we bolt towards her in the hallway.

“Hi, Jilly. Um, I know we had some confusion about me trying to get attention, and that’s not true. Before I went on the field, I asked to borrow your extra stick, well…um…I think that stick was mine,” I quickly give a weak smile.

Jilly just looks at me like I’m crazy. “Ugh! You really think I would steal your stupid stick?!” she says rudely. “You’re a bigger snob then I thought!! And I do not accept your apology for being so rude to me! You are like, so stupid! Why don’t you just get another injury and blame it on me! You big mean person!” Then before I can say another word, she runs off and starts telling everyone I am a bigger snob than she thought I was. She also is saying I accused her of stealing my “stupid stick.”

“Great, I’m just trying to ask a polite thing, and she puts words in my mouth! Now, I’ll never find my stick!” I start to get discouraged.

“Well, Kira, we know who stole your stick!” Ana points out.

“Mysterious voice!!!” my face lights up.

“Yeah! Now, who *is* Mysterious Voice?”

“I don’t know or wait! Maybe I do…,” I think.

“Let’s talk at lunch,” Ana says while running towards first period.

Finally, lunch arrives.

"Boy, I'm hungry!" I say while pulling out a delicious ham and cheese sandwich.

"Yeah, me too. But remember, we have to figure out who this Mysterious Voice is. Ideas, we need ideas," Ana says and looks at me.

"What?" I stop.

"Who is the one who lied to our faces?" Ana starts getting mysterious herself.

"I don't—JILLY!! But she said she didn't do it. AND, why would she do it? Plus, how could my brother Toby, be working for her? He is seventeen, she's ten!" I state.

"She also made rumors about you, and she's jealous of you! I bet you, she made Toby be Mysterious Voice!" Ana replies.

"Ahh! You're on to something now! But, why would my brother listen to her?" I ask curiously.

"Because, um…" Ana begins.

But then it all makes sense.

"Because of that picture! Remember? The one of Toby at age 12. On Halloween he was Princess Laya! I showed Jilly that picture! She probably stole that picture, and threatened Toby to show everyone that picture unless he worked for her! It all makes sense! It was Toby with the black cloak. In his room, he gave the description of Jilly! Let's go get her, Ana!" I hold out my hand and ask, "Are you in?" I wait patiently for a response.

"Yes!" Ana responds excitedly (but not so sure), while she has her hand on top of mine. So after we finish eating our delicious sandwiches, we run once again into Jilly. But this time, I am full of confidence and have a witness.

"Ugh! Now what snob," Jilly smirked while turning towards my former teammates.

"We know you stole my stick," I say, a little loudly.

"Oh, this again. I have no idea what you're talking about! Now, for the last time go away!" Jilly chuckles while she turns away back towards her cell phone.

"Let's see, talking to snobby girl. Keeps accusing me of taking her stupid stick! LOL!" Jilly read her text out loud. "And, send!"

Bleep! Bleep! Bleep! went everyone's phone. Everybody now has their eyes on me and Jilly. "Way to make everyone stop and stare, Jilly." I can feel my face getting warm. My cheeks are flushed.

"Oh, is Miss Perfect getting so scared and nervous? Hmm?" Jilly asks sarcastically.

"Um…um…" I stutter.

Ana gives me a boost. "What she means is, well, she really thinks you stole her stick. Did you?" Ana spits out and then goes behind me.

"Jilly, before this whole commotion happened, remember when we were best friends? I would do anything for you! And you would do anything for me! I miss that friend, a lot. What ever happened to her?" I stand up for myself.

There is yet again another awkward moment of silence. Jilly looks down at her shoes. I know I have her then. So I continue, "Back in second grade, you were so sweet and nice. We were like sisters. Just like sisters you would always say. And now you are acting strangely and dishonestly. Why?"

"Oh! So now I am rude and mean? And yet again, I didn't steal your dumb stick!"

Jilly was so close to returning to nice Jilly, but once again, she turns back into rude Jilly. I hate it when she puts words in my mouth.

"If you love your stick so much, why don't you marry it? Oh wait!

You are too lousy for that thing! No wonder it got lost!" Jilly fake laughs. I don't like it when rude girls fake laugh. It is so obnoxious. But that explains why Jilly does it.

I swallow hard, thinking positive energy and thoughts and say, "Jilly, why do you keep lying to me? I know you did it! Why are you acting so rude?" I kind of snap. Then, things get real.

"You listen to me one last time. I didn't do it!!! Do I have to spell it out to your little brain, jerk! I did not steal your stupid, dumb stick! Since you are so hopeless, you just HAVE to blame me! Well too bad! I may have manipulated your dumb brother to get him to scare you, and I also may have made that stick too long so you would get injured so I could get the jersey. I may have started rumors so everyone wouldn't like you, but I didn't steal that disgusting thing you call your lucky charm. I also might have made your brother be my assistant for a month because of his embarrassing picture. But..." she stops talking because by now everyone is staring, even teachers. She is screaming that loudly.

"Do you hate me that much?!" I ask before I start crying from total embarrassment and hop on my crutches into the girl's bathroom. I do not want anyone to see me cry, so I decide to just go to the bathroom. I am as embarrassed as a kid in her underwear in front of school. Ana runs right after me, but first she stopped to tell Jilly something.

"You know what Jilly? Kira is the best of the best when it comes to friends! Anybody with a nice big brain would know how lucky it is to have a friend like her! But no! You just had to hurt her because you got so jealous that I came back. You couldn't take it! You had your chance to have a great friend, but it looks like you blew it. So, I am sorry for you," Ana looks at her dead in the eye, shakes her head, and turns away to go to the bathroom.

Everyone is now staring at Jilly; her are cheeks flushed. She looks down at her shoes again.

"Jilly Tent, please report to the principal's office. Now!!" a screechy loud voice screams. For your information, I think it was the principal.

And she does not seem happy. Underline not. She must have heard the commotion as well.

"Kira? Kira? Where are you?" Ana commands politely.

"I'm not here," I sob. Then I open the door, and she hugs me. "Thanks," I show a weak smile.

Chapter 5

Finale

"ARE YOU OK NOW?" ANA ASKS. "JILLY WAS REALLY ROUGH ON YOU. She has a lot of issues! And I remember she was so like, nice to everyone! I do not know what has gotten into her ever since second grade. I gave her a little talk. You are welcome. I don't know why she still lies to our faces! She must be super jealous! Does she know all of us could be friends? I mean, right? It would be rude to only hang out with one person. She seems a little too desperate, if she is that jealous! But that explains Jilly: rude, with a dash of desperate personality. I don't know why she can't just drop it! She has been holding a grudge for like three long, years! But, the good news is the principal told her to be in her office! Poor Jilly! Yeah right! This is her fault, and she deserves a punishment."

We both look at each other.

Meanwhile, in the principal's office:

"Um, Mrs. Dess. You wanted to see me," a scared Jilly closes the door slowly, full of fear.

"Yes, please. Sit down," a very unhappy principal snaps while motioning towards the small red seat.

She probably doesn't have visitors that often, or else this place would be friendlier looking! Jilly thinks as she sits down.

"It seems that there was some commotion in the hallway with you and Kira. I thought you two were best friends. I am so disappointed. Remember that card you two made for me?" She points towards the small card on her big gigantic desk. It is covered in scribbles.

"Wow. I must have messed up. I remember that card. We promised to always be friends. Wow. What did I do? I screwed up, badly. I need to say sorry to Kira, and Toby. And I need to face the consequences. And make everything right."

After a moment of silence, Mrs. Dess interrupts Jilly while she is in very deep thought. "Miss Tent, please explain what all this commotion is all about involving you and Kira," Mrs. Dess demands.

"Well…you see, I got jealous because Kira's smart, pretty, and talented in lacrosse, and umm…I…sort of," Jilly stumbles with her words.

"You did what? Please, continue with what you were saying," Mrs. Dess seems interested.

"Ok, I made rumors about her! When we were little, we were best friends! But then when Ana came back, it felt like I was left out!"

"And did you ever tell her that?" Mrs. Dess interrupted again.

"No…" Jilly mumbles. "Anyway, I could not keep all of that anger that had been building up inside me, and I just exploded. I made some rumors, made her scared, and hurt her. And now that I think about it, I was really cruel and rotten to her. Then…" Jilly's words trailed off.

"Then what?" Mrs. Dess asks, like a kid wanting to know about a fairy tale.

"Then, I tried to freak her out by being a 'Mysterious Voice' and took her stick. Then I denied that I took it when she asked me. Then, I screamed at her and made her cry. I know I need a big punishment, and I owe her a huge apology. And I need to never do it again. AND I should give her back her lacrosse stick, with a big apology and a hug," Jilly felt really, truly sorry. *Wow. I seriously messed up! No wonder she cried, and no wonder I am going to get in so much trouble! I would not blame Kira if she does not except my apology! I know I would definitely not forgive me, that is for sure!* Jilly thought quietly to herself.

"Yes, indeed. You need to do all your duties. Starting with an apology to both Kira and Toby. You know, I am happy you realized you messed up, and you will learn from your mistakes. But first, you must be punished, and you must apologize." Then, Mrs. Dess handed Jilly a hot pink slip. It read, "Detention every Wednesday for eight weeks and a demerit." Then Mrs. Dess picks up the phone and calls Jilly's mom.

I deserve it, I made this big commotion happen, and I need to end it and face the punishment, Jilly thinks with her head hung with sadness.

"I know; I screwed up pretty badly. Thank you, Mrs. Dess, and I am sorry for screwing up," Jilly holds her head up high, as she quickly stands up. But before she can leave, Mrs. Dess interrupts Jilly once again.

But can Jilly argue? *No. You should not be rude,* Jilly thinks.

"Um...wait one moment Jilly. I was watching the game, and you are really talented in lacrosse. And you are really smart, and pretty. Do not put yourself down like that. You were probably feeling discouraged, and you got upset. The same thing happened to me. And did you know, when I was twenty-two, I won a national lacrosse tournament!? I even got accepted into Yale! If you set your mind on something, you can achieve it!" Mrs. Dess encourages Jilly.

"Wow. Congratulations, Mrs. Dess, and thank you for all that encouragement. It really will make me think before I act or speak."

Right after Mrs. Dess dismisses Jilly, she runs straight to the girl's bathroom to apologize. Jilly breathes in and opens the bathroom door. "Hello? Kira? Are you in here? I'm such a jerk. I'm so sorry. I was Mysterious Voice, and a big fat meany. Here is your stick. I was just jealous of you because you're pretty, and smart, and have friends, and are good at lacrosse, unlike me. I didn't mean to hurt your feelings. I was just upset because I, I miss you as my friend. I was just upset that you and Ana became friends," Jilly tried to open the bathroom stall.

"Really? Is that true Jilly?" I sob opening the door again.

"Absolutely. I'm so sorry!" Jilly says while handing me my lucky stick and giving me a hug.

"That's ok," I say hugging her back. "And you're pretty, and smart, and have friends, and are good at lacrosse too! We can all be friends! Together!" I say encouraging Jilly.

"Really?" she asks surprised.

"Definitely," I say confidently.

About KidPub Press

KidPub is devoted to helping kids develop their writing skills by giving them a safe, fun, supportive place to express their creativity. At KidPub we understand that kids have great ideas and plenty of stories to tell.

In addition to our web site, we publish books, like this one, written by kids of all ages. You can find many more books to enjoy, written by young authors, in our online bookstore at http://bookstore.kidpub.com.

Thousands of visitors come each day to KidPub to read the stories posted by our members, and to post their own writing. We invite you to visit KidPub, browse our books, read new stories, and find out how you can publish your own book with KidPub Press. We're on the web at www.kidpub.com.

16713113R10017

Made in the USA
Charleston, SC
07 January 2013